Shoo!

For Elsie and Emile
M.R.

For the children of
Brantfield Nursery School, Kendal
J.L.

First published in paperback in Great Britain by HarperCollins Children's Books in 2007
ISBN-13: 978-0-00-722556-9
ISBN-10: 0-00-722556-3
1 3 5 7 9 10 8 6 4 2
HarperCollins Children's Books is a division of HarperCollins Publishers Ltd.
Text copyright © Michael Rosen 2007
Illustrations copyright © Jonathan Langley 2007
The author and illustrator assert the moral right to be identified as the author and illustrator of the work.
A CIP catalogue record for this title is available from the British Library.

Visit our website at: www.harpercollinschildrensbooks.co.uk
Printed in China

Shoo!

Michael Rosen
illustrated by
Jonathan Langley

HarperCollins *Children's Books*

It was very hot.

Pig and all the Piglets, Dog, Cow,

Sheep and Cat were in the barn.

'Miaow!' thought Cat. 'I'd be cooler on my own.

I'll chase all the other animals away!'

So Cat went up
to Pig and all the Piglets.

SHOO! he said.

Pig and all the Piglets didn't much like that. They scampered out of the barn.

Then Cat went up to Dog.

SHOO! he said.

Woof!

Dog didn't much like that.
He jumped up and ran out of the barn.

Then Cat went up to
Cow and Sheep.

SHOOOOO!!

he said.

Cow and Sheep
didn't like that
at all.

Moo!

Baa!

Baa!

They galloped
out of the barn.

'Purr!' said Cat.
'Now I've got the
barn all to myself.'

Outside, Pig and all the Piglets, Dog, Cow and Sheep met Donkey.

'Cat just chased us out of the barn!' said Dog.

'Chase?' said one of the Piglets.
'Hey! Let's play chase!'

So the animals pretended to be Cat and chased each other.

Everyone was having such a good time.

'I'm all alone,' Cat thought. 'Why won't anyone play with me?'

'Miaow!' he called.
'Do you want to come back in the barn?'

The animals stopped running about.
'No thanks!' said Dog.
'Too hot in there,'
said Cow.

'We're having a good time out here!'
said all the others...

...and they started playing chase again.

'I wish I hadn't said Shoo to everyone!'
Cat thought.
One of the Piglets peeped in the barn.

'Why don't you
come outside and
play chase with us?'
said the Piglet.

'Miaow – really?'
said Cat.

And he
bounced out
of the window…

...into the field.

Soon Pig and all the Piglets, Dog, Cow, Sheep, Donkey and Cat were running about all over the place.

Until it was time for bed. **Shhh!**

Books by Michael Rosen and Jonathan Langley:

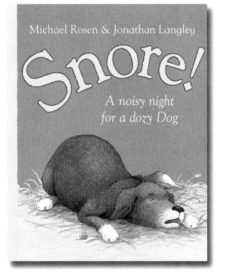

Paperback ISBN-13: 978-0-00-716031-0
Audio version available

Hardback ISBN-13: 978-0-00-712442-8
Paperback ISBN-13: 978-0-00-712443-5

Books by Jonathan Langley:

Hardback ISBN-13: 978-0-00-198292-5

Paperback ISBN-13: 978-0-00-664698-3

HarperCollins *Children's Books*